DANNY AND THE MERRY-GO-ROUND

by

Nan Holcomb

illustrated by
Virginia Lucia

JASON & NORDIC PUBLISHERS
HOLLIDAYSBURG, PENNSYLVANIA

Books in this series
DANNY AND THE MERRY-GO-ROUND
HOW ABOUT A HUG
ANDY FINDS A TURTLE

DANNY AND THE MERRY-GO-ROUND

Text copyright 1984 Nan Holcomb
Illustrations copyright 1987 Virginia Lucia

Library of Congress Cataloging in Publication Data

Holcomb, Nan, 1928-

Danny and the merry-go-round / by Nan Holcomb;
illustrated by Virginia Lucia.
p. cm.

Summary: Danny, who has cerebral palsy, is faced with another frustrating day at the playground watching the other children play, until a friendly gesture from another kid gives him an unexpected adventure and helps him feel better about himself.

ISBN 0-944727-11-5

(1. Cerebral palsy—Fiction. 2. Physically handicapped—Fiction. 3. Self—acceptance—Fiction.) I. Lucia, Virginia, ill. II. Title. PZ7.H6972Dan 1987

(E)—dc19   87-29772
                                                                                                    CIP
Printed in the U.S.A.

Dedicated to Stacey Benton,
a girl like Liz

The sun felt warm on Danny's face. A fat gray squirrel with a bushy tail peeked around a clump of flowers at the corner of the street.

Mom pushed Danny's chair to a bench near the playground so he could watch the children play.

Danny didn't like to watch them play.
Sitting in his same old chair
wasn't any fun at all—not
when other kids were swinging and
riding the merry-go-round or
whizzing down the slide.

$\mathbb{D}$anny watched the little red-haired girl climb up-up-up, step over and scream as she flashed down the slide and banged her bottom into the dirt at the end of the slide.

Danny looked down at his hand
and watched a lady bug
crawl over his thumb.
"That's a pretty lady bug."
Danny looked up and the little
red-haired girl smiled at him.

"Why don't you come and slide down the slide?" the little girl asked.

Danny squinted his eyes at her. Boy, didn't she know anything? He couldn't slide. He just sat and watched.

Mom smiled and said, "Danny can't slide down the slide because he can't climb up or hang on or even sit well enough to slide down it."

"How come?" the little red-haired girl asked.

"Because he has had cerebral palsy since he was born."

The little girl moved away
from Danny.

Danny closed his eyes.

"It's not a sickness like a cold,"
Mommy said. "Nobody can
catch cerebral palsy. A little part of
Danny's brain doesn't work quite right.
His legs and arms just don't get the
message to move the way
he would like them to."

Danny looked at his mother. Was he surprised! No one had ever told him that before. They just said, "Move this or hold up your head, open your hand, relax." Then he'd get discouraged because nothing happened.

"Mm-mm," Danny hummed and looked at his hands. He tried extra hard to lift them high. One hand went up high—well, quite high. The other stayed still in his lap.

"Oh," the little red-haired girl said and stared into Danny's face. "That's OK. I like you anyway, Danny. My name is Liz."

Вut then she ran away!
Danny watched her run down the hill.
He felt sad. He hunted all over his lap for the ladybug, but she'd flown away, too. He closed his eyes.

Soon he heard, "Danny, Danny. Look who's here!"

Danny looked up. The little red-haired girl was pulling a big red-haired man up the walk.

"You can go on the slide and the swing and the merry-go-round! My Daddy will help you."

"Maybe not the slide," the man said, "But, we could try the merry-go-round. How does that sound?"

Mommy smiled. "Well, Danny? Shall we give it a try?"

Liz and her Dad got behind Danny's chair and off they all went to the merry-go-round.

Liz jumped on the merry-go-round and stuck her feet straight out. Mommy sat on the merry-go-round and waited for Liz's Daddy to put Danny beside her.

Danny felt scared. He'd fall and the thing would gobble him up!

"Hey, Dan," the man said and held him tight. "Don't be afraid. We won't let you fall."

Gently he bent Dan's legs
and put him next to Mommy. She
helped Danny hold on to the bar and the
merry-go-round began to turn.

Danny wanted to scream, "Let me out
of here!" Then he looked at Liz.
She had her head back and was laughing
as the wind blew her hair.

Dan held himself straight,
put his head back as far as possible so
the wind would blow in his face.

The merry-go-round went faster and
faster and Dan wasn't afraid.

He laughed and the wind blew his hair.